For Titita, Rafael, Michael, and Erika.

I AM PANGOO THE PENGUIN

SATOMI ICHIKAWA

Philomel Books

I love Danny and Danny loves me.

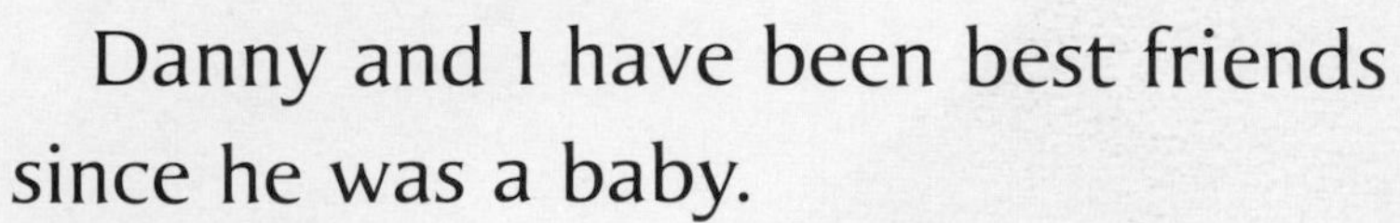

Danny and I have been best friends since he was a baby.

We always play together, eat together and sleep together.

What we love is going to the Central Park Children's Zoo together.

Grandma takes us every Saturday. We especially love to watch the penguins swimming.

One day, many people come to the house. Grandma comes, too.

Everyone eats and sings: “Happy birthday, Danny!”

Danny is so busy that I hide behind a chair and only peek at what they are doing.

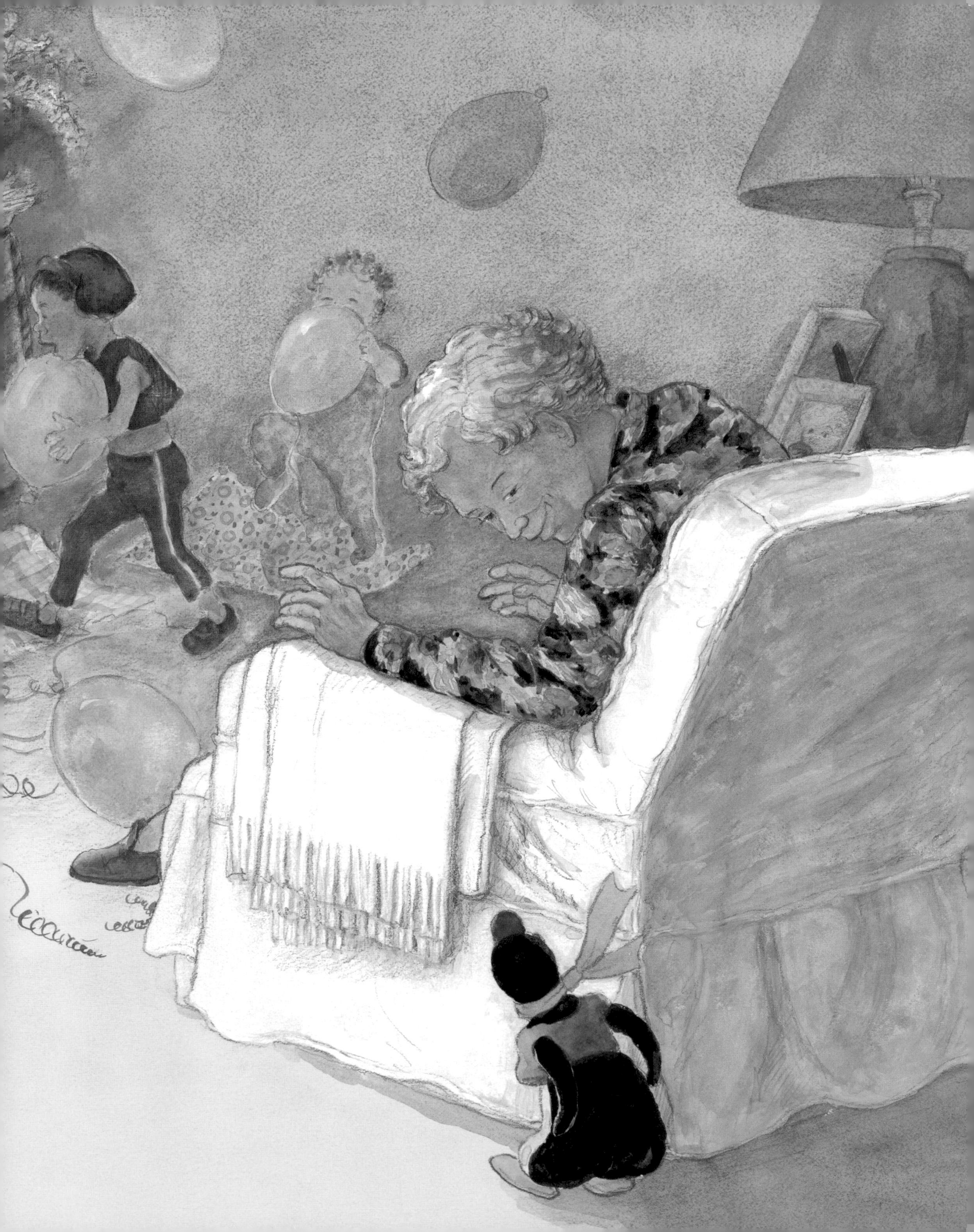

In the evening, Danny goes to bed, holding all of his brand-new animals in his arms.

Oh, Danny, how about me? But he forgets me.

For the first time in my life, I spend a dark night alone.

I wake up in the morning. I am still alone. I am certain Danny doesn't love me anymore. I feel sad.

Wait! I am a penguin. There are penguins in the zoo. Maybe I belong with them.

I slip away through the window.
I am going to see them. Absolutely!

35

ONE WAY

I finally arrive at the zoo.
But where are the penguins? I can't remember!
Then I hear music. I know where it comes from.

From the animals on the clock tower!

"Are you looking for something?" a penguin with a drum asks me.

He will know.

I say, "Yes! I am looking for the penguins!"

"They are right over there. Go and see and say hello for me," he says.

I go straight there.

Here they are! Penguins! Like me!

From the other side of the window, the penguins swim to see me.

"Hello," I say to them, "I am Pangoo the penguin."

"You, a penguin? You do not look like us!" one says.

"Do you like living in the cold?" another says.

"No . . ." I say.

"Do you eat fish?"

"Never," I say.

"Do you swim?"

I shake my head no.
So the penguins swim away gracefully.
I am sure I don't know how to swim like they do.
I cannot belong with them.

But if I don't belong with them, where do I belong?
I am alone again, and nobody loves me.

Black Tie Optional

Suddenly, I hear a voice calling my name.

"Pangoo! Pangoo!"

It's Danny and Grandma!

"Oh, Pangoo, I looked everywhere for you. Grandma thought you would come here and she was right. I am so glad that I have found you.

"I love you, Pangoo. Don't ever go away!"

I hear music from the clock tower.

The penguin with a drum calls out, "Did you find what you were looking for?"

"Yes, I did," I say.

Tonight Danny holds me tight in his arm when he goes to bed.

And me? I am happy. I know just where I belong.

Patricia Lee Gauch, editor

PHILOMEL BOOKS
A division of Penguin Young Readers Group.
Published by The Penguin Group.
Penguin Group (USA) Inc., 375 Hudson Street, New York, NY 10014, U.S.A.
Penguin Group (Canada), 90 Eglinton Avenue East, Suite 700, Toronto, Ontario, Canada M4P 2Y3
(a division of Pearson Penguin Canada Inc.).
Penguin Books Ltd, 80 Strand, London WC2R 0RL, England.
Penguin Ireland, 25 St. Stephen's Green, Dublin 2, Ireland (a division of Penguin Books Ltd.).
Penguin Group (Australia), 250 Camberwell Road, Camberwell, Victoria 3124, Australia
(a division of Pearson Australia Group Pty Ltd).
Penguin Books India Pvt Ltd, 11 Community Centre, Panchsheel Park, New Delhi - 110 017, India.
Penguin Group (NZ), Cnr Airborne and Rosedale Roads, Albany, Auckland 1310, New Zealand
(a division of Pearson New Zealand Ltd).
Penguin Books (South Africa) (Pty) Ltd, 24 Sturdee Avenue, Rosebank, Johannesburg 2196, South Africa.
Penguin Books Ltd, Registered Offices: 80 Strand, London WC2R 0RL, England.

Published simultaneously in Canada. Manufactured in China by South China Printing Co. Ltd.

Design by Semadar Megged. Text set in 17-point Grantofte Regular.
The art was done in watercolor.

Library of Congress Cataloging-in-Publication Data
Ichikawa, Satomi. I am Pangoo the penguin / Satomi Ichikawa. p. cm.
Summary: Feeling neglected when Danny goes to sleep with his new stuffed animals rather than with him,
Pangoo runs away to the zoo to live with the real-life penguins.
[1. Penguins—Fiction. 2. Toys—Fiction. 3. Zoos—Fiction.] I. Title. PZ7.I16Pan 2006 [E]—dc22 2005032640

ISBN 0-399-23313-X
1 3 5 7 9 10 8 6 4 2
First Impression